Dear Parent:

Congratulations! Your child is taking the first steps on an exciting journey. The destination? Independent reading!

STEP INTO READING® will help your child get there. The program offers books at five levels that accompany children from their first attempts at reading to reading success. Each step includes fun stories, fiction and nonfiction, and colorful art. There are also Step into Reading Sticker Books, Step into Reading Math Readers, and Step into Reading Phonics Readers— a complete literacy program with something to interest every child.

Learning to Read, Step by Step!

Ready to Read Preschool–Kindergarten
• big type and easy words • rhyme and rhythm • picture clues
For children who know the alphabet and are eager to begin reading.

Reading with Help Preschool–Grade 1
• basic vocabulary • short sentences • simple stories
For children who recognize familiar words and sound out new words with help.

Reading on Your Own Grades 1–3
• engaging characters • easy-to-follow plots • popular topics
For children who are ready to read on their own.

Reading Paragraphs Grades 2–3
• challenging vocabulary • short paragraphs • exciting stories
For newly independent readers who read simple sentences with confidence.

Ready for Chapters Grades 2–4
• chapters • longer paragraphs • full-color art
For children who want to take the plunge into chapter books but still like colorful pictures.

STEP INTO READING® is designed to give every child a successful reading experience. The grade levels are only guides. Children can progress through the steps at their own speed, developing confidence in their reading, no matter what their grade.

Remember, a lifetime love of reading starts with a single step!

For Kevin, with love
—M.L.

www.stepintoreading.com

Educators and librarians, for a variety of teaching tools, visit us at
www.randomhouse.com/teachers

Library of Congress Cataloging-in-Publication Data
Lagonegro, Melissa.
Home, stinky home / by Melissa Lagonegro.
   p. cm. — (Step into reading. A step 2 book)
Summary: Lilo and Stitch find the perfect home for a very stinky alien.
ISBN 0-7364-2240-4 — ISBN 0-7364-8031-5 (lib. bdg.)
[1. Extraterrestrial beings — Fiction.] I. Title. II. Step into reading. Step 2 book.
PZ7.L14317Ho 2004 — [E] — dc22 2003012411

Printed in the United States of America   10 9 8 7 6 5 4 3

STEP INTO READING, RANDOM HOUSE, and the Random House colophon are registered trademarks
and the Step into Reading colophon is a trademark of Random House, Inc

DISNEY'S
Lilo & Stitch
The Series

Home, Stinky Home

By Melissa Lagonegro
Illustrated by Carlo Lo Raso

Random House 🏠 New York

Lilo and Stitch
had to find
a nice home
for Alien 254.
And keep him
away from Gantu!

The little alien
was pink.
He was furry.
He had big eyes!

"You are so cute!"
said Lilo.

Even Myrtle and
the girls liked him!

"This little guy
is helping me make
friends," said Lilo.

But the alien
had a secret.
He was a ticking
stink bomb!
"Oh, my!" said Pleakley.

Lilo still wanted
to keep him.
"I am naming
you Mr. Stenchy."

"Arrgghh!" said Stitch.

He was mad.

Lilo took Mr. Stenchy
to a tea party.
Stitch came, too.
He made a big mess.
<u>Bang</u>! <u>Crash</u>!

"You should act more like Mr. Stenchy," said Lilo. That made Stitch <u>really</u> mad.

Lilo had to go
to the store.
"Stitch, you are
in charge,"
she said.

"Roo, roo!"
said Mr. Stenchy.
He wanted to play.
But Stitch did not
want to play!

Crash!

Gantu broke into
the house.
He came to take
Mr. Stenchy away.

"He is mine!"
said Gantu.

Now Stitch was happy.

Lilo came home.

Oh, no!

Mr. Stenchy was gone.

Lilo was sad.

"Now Mr. Stenchy
will never find a
real home," she said.

Stitch felt bad.

He wanted to make

Lilo happy again.

So he went to get

Mr. Stenchy back.

"We have to help
Stitch!" said Lilo.
"Let's go!"

The friends worked
as a team to get
Mr. Stenchy back.

"Come to us," said Lilo.

"Come to me," said Gantu.

Suddenly . . .

. . . Mr. Stenchy
started to stink!

"Pee-yew!" said Lilo.

"Eeega!" said Stitch.

"Yuck!" said Gantu.

"Take him away!"

"Mmmm," said Pleakley. "This is a lovely smell on my planet."

Lilo had an idea.
"I know the
perfect home for
Mr. Stenchy,"
she said.

Pleakley's planet!